Aldo
Applesauce

Weekly Reader Books presents

Aldo Applesauce

Johanna Hurwitz

ILLUSTRATED BY JOHN WALLNER

William Morrow and Company
New York 1979

Copyright © 1979 by Johanna Hurwitz

Library of Congress Cataloging in Publication Data

Hurwitz, Johanna.

Aldo Applesauce.
Summary: When he and his family move to the suburbs, Aldo
has difficulty finding new friends.
[1. Moving, Household—Fiction. 2. Friendship—Fiction]
I. Wallner, John C. II. Title.
PZ7.H9574Al [Fic] 79-16200
ISBN 0-688-22199-8
ISBN 0-688-32199-2 lib. bdg.

Printed in the United States of America.

For Connie and Libby,
yesterday, today, and tomorrow.

Contents

CHAPTER ONE

The House
on Hillside La

It was bedtime and the light was out.

Aldo Sossi lay in bed trying to fall asleep. The bed was his old one, but the bedroom was new. This morning the Sossi family had moved from New York City to Woodside, New Jersey. There were so many thoughts jumping about in Aldo's head that he couldn't relax and go to sleep. Tomorrow he would start attending the fourth grade at the Woodside School.

"Nobody moves and starts a new school in the middle of the year," Elaine, his older sister, had complained to their parents.

"This is January fifth," Mr. Sossi had answered. "It's not exactly the middle of the year."

But for the Sossi children, Elaine and Karen and Aldo, the year seemed to begin when school opened in September. Having their father change jobs and make the family move in January seemed very difficult.

Actually, when Mr. Sossi had told his children about the proposed move to New Jersey, it had seemed very exciting. Elaine and Karen, who were fourteen and twelve and a half, were delighted that they were going to have their own private rooms. Their mother promised the children that they could invite their old city friends to come and sleep over when there was a school vacation. And they liked the thought of living in their own house and having a backyard, an upstairs and a downstairs, a fireplace, and an attic.

Aldo remembered the Saturday about a month ago when the family had driven out to visit their new home. It was located on Hillside La, which seemed odd since the area was actually on level ground. The real address was 17 Hillside Lane. *La* was an abbreviation, and all the street signs they passed used the short form: Forest La, Maple La, Cherry La, and finally their own Hillside La.

"*Quelle maison!*" shouted Elaine, when the car stopped. She was studying French this year at school, and she liked to use French words whenever she could. Mrs. Sossi had studied French years ago but had forgotten it all. So no one could be sure what Elaine was saying, and if she sometimes made a mistake, no one could correct her.

Aldo noticed with pleasure that their new house was really several houses. First, there was the house that they would all live in. Then there was a garage, which was the house for the car. In the city they had just parked the car out on the street. There was also a dog-house in the yard, and finally, hanging from an old maple tree, there was a little birdhouse.

"Will we get a dog to live in the doghouse?" Aldo had asked his parents eagerly. Aldo loved animals, and he had wanted a dog for as long as he could remember.

"I don't know. Let's wait and see how things work out," said his mother. "Maybe the cats will want the house for themselves," she said. The Sossi family had two cats, Peabody and Poughkeepsie.

"Will the cats go outdoors?" wondered Karen. In the city the cats were always kept inside the apartment. Life in the suburbs was obviously going to mean a lot of changes for them all, even the cats.

They had gone inside, and each of the Sossi children had picked out a bedroom. It was fun walking through the empty rooms and hearing their voices echoing as they called out their discoveries to one another.

"*Voila!*" Elaine shouted. "This room has a window seat!"

Karen found a closet that was so big it had a window inside it.

Aldo was interested in everything. He went down to the basement, where there was a furnace and a washing machine and a dryer. He investigated the attic, which had nothing in it but dust and old spider webs.

Mrs. Sossi was mentally moving all their furniture about. "Let's put the sofa here." She pointed to one area of the living room. "And we can put the television over here."

It had been a very exciting day, and Aldo, watching squirrels chase one another up and down the maple tree in the backyard, had tried not to think how nervous he would feel when the time came to start the new school.

The month in between had gone very quickly. Now he tossed in his bed and wished that they had never moved at all. He wondered if he would have a good teacher. He worried that the things this new fourth grade was studying would be different from what he had been learning back at P.S. 35. And he worried about making new friends.

Suddenly Aldo heard the door to his bedroom squeak open. His father had said that he would have to put oil on some of the hinges.

15

Now the noise was like the scary sound effects they used on television or in the movies. Something landed with a thud on Aldo's bed. But even though it was too dark to see, he knew what it was and he wasn't frightened.

Either Peabody or Poughkeepsie had come to sleep on his bed. Aldo wished he could see in the dark, like the cats. Then he could tell which one had come to spend the night with him. It didn't matter, though. He loved them both equally. He thought of them as if they were his brothers or his best friends. He had given them secret nicknames that no one else in his family knew: Peeps and Pouks.

"How do you like it here?" he whispered to the cat. And as if in answer, the cat began a very soft purr.

The pressure of the cat's body cuddling up against his feet comforted Aldo, and he began to relax.

"Good night, Puss," he whispered affectionately, as he started to fall asleep. Maybe tomorrow wouldn't be so bad after all.

CHAPTER TWO

Off to School

When Aldo opened the front door of their house the next morning, a bright-red Volkswagen car was passing down Hillside Lane. Aldo quickly turned to Elaine, who was standing behind him, and squeezed her arm through her winter jacket.

"Red Volks!" he shouted. In his old neighborhood, the car had been a good-luck charm, and all the kids vied with one another to see who could shout out the magic words first. The idea was to pinch someone, say "Red Volks," and make a wish. Aldo was never sure

19

if it worked or not, but if ever he needed luck, this was the day.

"Oh, Aldo! Are you still playing that baby game?" Elaine said to her brother scornfully. Even though she and Karen were entering a new school today too, they both seemed very calm. Aldo wondered if he would feel different if he were going to junior high school like his sisters. He doubted it. They had both eaten their breakfast, even though he had hardly swallowed a bite.

The new school was exactly three blocks away. Aldo walked with his mother. Elaine and Karen were lucky. They had to take a bus to the junior high school, and they looked very grown up waving good-bye as they stood at the bus stop. On the other hand, Aldo wasn't sure that he would want to walk into a new school alone. His mother took him into the school office. It looked very much like the office in P.S. 35.

Aldo stood looking at the little mailboxes

with all the teachers' names as his mother explained to the secretary at the main desk that her son's records had been sent here. Aldo counted four rows of mailboxes with ten boxes in each row. Forty teachers. He wondered which one he would have.

The secretary told Aldo to sit down, and she took some papers into another office. Outside the office, boys and girls were walking back and forth. Aldo heard the bell ring and watched them rushing to their classrooms. The secretary returned and told Mrs. Sossi that everything had been arranged. She could go home now.

"Will you know how to get home again?" his mother asked. "I can come and pick you up at three o'clock."

Aldo blushed. His mother hadn't come to school for him since he finished first grade.

"I know the way," he said, hoping that he did. Three o'clock and going-home time seemed awfully far off.

Aldo's mother started to bend down to kiss Aldo good-bye. Aldo's eyes filled with apprehension. Suddenly his mother seemed to remember that her son was nine going on ten. She straightened up again and patted his shoulder. "Have a good day," she said. No kiss!

Maybe he would have a good day and maybe he wouldn't. He would know at three o'clock. Aldo smiled at his mother and followed the secretary down the hall.

"There are four fourth grades," she said. "You are going to have Mrs. Moss. She's a fine teacher."

Aldo nodded. It was nice of the secretary to try and reassure him. Moss reminded Aldo of the soft, green ground covering he sometimes found in the park. It was a good name. He liked it better than Nesse, which was the name of his old teacher back at P.S. 35.

Mrs. Moss was speaking to the class when Aldo entered with the secretary. Everyone turned to look at Aldo. It was the moment

he had dreaded most. The secretary whispered to Mrs. Moss, and Aldo tried to look at the other children without letting them see how nervous he felt. There were no rows in this classroom. The students sat around tables. Six tables with four chairs at a table, Aldo counted. That would make twenty-four students if all the chairs were taken. He noticed that a few were empty.

Mrs. Moss turned to the class. "This is Aldo Sossi. Welcome to our class, Aldo," she said. "DeDe, raise your hand," she instructed. "Aldo, you can sit at the table next to DeDe." Aldo turned to the girl whose arm was raised. He wished he didn't have to sit next to a girl.

Aldo looked back to Mrs. Moss as she continued speaking to him. Something about that girl DeDe had been peculiar, and he tried to remember what he had seen. He turned to look again at the table where she sat, and as he walked toward her he realized what it was.

DeDe was the only girl in the class with a large, black moustache.

CHAPTER THREE

A Fuss
in the Lunchroom

Aldo sat in his seat and pretended to pay attention. The lesson was on homophones. His old class had already studied about *their, there,* and *they're* last month. It would be super if he was a few weeks ahead in everything here, but he doubted it. On one wall of the room there was a chart of the solar system, and Aldo didn't know much about that.

He tried to look at the children in the class without turning his head. He wanted Mrs. Moss to think he was paying attention. Aldo listened to her calling on various students. There seemed to be an Allan and an Albert in the class. Also a Michael, two Davids, and two Peters. Aldo had never been in a class with another Aldo. The only one he had ever known was his uncle Aldo. He didn't pay much attention to the names of the girls. The only one who interested him was DeDe with her black moustache.

No one else seemed to think she was unusual. They acted as though she was an ordinary girl. Maybe if he had always had such a girl in his class, Aldo wouldn't have noticed her either. But as it was, he decided she must be a freak. She belonged in the circus.

Aldo was so busy with his thoughts that he was scarcely aware Mrs. Moss was going on with the lesson. "There are two boys named David in this class. How do you spell *there* in that sentence, Allan? Oh, no, I mean Aldo. Aldo Sossi."

Aldo heard his name and started to attention. He was about to ask her to repeat the question when he heard a voice behind him chant, "Oh, no, Aldo."

Mrs. Moss repeated the question, but Aldo still didn't hear. He turned a bright red as he heard the whispered voice chanting, "Oh, no, Aldo. Oh, no, Aldo."

"Pay attention, Aldo. It is very important to learn all these words," said Mrs. Moss. "DeDe, what is the answer?"

Underneath her moustache, DeDe grinned. "*T-h-e-r-e*," she spelled correctly.

It had been Aldo's chance to prove that he was smart, and he had goofed it. He looked at DeDe. With relief he saw that one end of her moustache was coming away from her lip. It wasn't real at all. She pressed it to her skin, and it stuck fast again. Maybe before the day was out he could discover the mystery of the moustache.

When it was lunchtime, Aldo grabbed his lunch box and followed everyone down the hall. Aldo's class was on the second lunch shift, which meant that they ate from twelve to twelve thirty and then had recess until one o'clock. The schedule was explained to him by Mrs. Moss. The class marched down the hall in an orderly line, but as they reached the lunchroom door, the line suddenly broke. Then there was a wild scramble as boys and girls pushed one another for a chance to sit next to their friends. Mrs. Moss turned her head and pretended not to notice. She was on her lunch hour, and the students were now the responsibility of the parent aides.

The room smelled exactly like the lunchroom in his old school—of old peanut-butter and tuna-fish sandwiches. There were long tables, and each class had its assigned area.

Aldo wondered where he should sit. He would have liked to have made friends with Allan or Albert, but their end of the table was already filled.

"Want to sit here?" called DeDe. Aldo would have preferred a boy, but at least someone wanted him. He sat down.

Aldo watched DeDe unpack her lunch and begin drinking milk through a straw. Her moustache pushed up on her lip, and she pulled it off and put it in her pocket. No one else seemed to think she was strange, and that in itself was the strangest thing of all, thought Aldo.

He opened his lunch box and removed his sandwich. Peanut butter. He almost always had peanut butter.

Aldo sniffed the air. "What kind of sandwich do you have?" he asked DeDe.

"Tuna fish."

"I thought so," said Aldo. "I don't eat tuna fish. First I didn't eat it because I became a vegetarian, and then my sister studied about dolphins in school and told me that they kill a lot of dolphins when they're fishing for the tuna fish. So now I have two reasons for not eating it."

"That's silly," said DeDe, reaching into her pocket for her moustache and putting it back under her nose.

Aldo wanted to say that nothing was so silly as a girl wearing a moustache, but he

30

didn't. She was the only person in the whole school who had bothered talking to him, and he was afraid of making her angry.

"What's a vegetarian?" DeDe asked.

"Someone who only eats vegetables and fruits and bread and stuff and who never eats meat. Or fish," Aldo added.

"You mean you don't have steak or chicken or anything like that?" asked DeDe with surprise.

"That's right," said Aldo proudly. "Chickens make me think of birds, and I like birds and other animals too much to eat them. I'm going to be a veterinarian when I grow up." He bit into his sandwich. "I eat lots of cheese and eggs and peanut butter," he said.

"Peanut-butter sandwiches are so dull," said DeDe. "I don't see how you could eat them all the time."

"My sister Elaine read in a library book that every year American children eat enough peanut butter to coat the Empire State Building with a layer three feet thick," said Aldo. "She said that I was probably responsible for one of those layers all by myself."

DeDe giggled. "I like animals too," she said. "I have a dog. She's a cocker spaniel. Her name is Cookie."

"I have two cats," said Aldo. "Peabody and Poughkeepsie."

Aldo reached into his lunch box and took out a little plastic container and a plastic spoon. He opened the container and started to eat the applesauce in it.

"We have a doghouse at my new house," he said. "Maybe we'll get a dog now, too."

As they were speaking, DeDe had leaned her chair back against the table behind them. Now she suddenly lost her balance and thrust out her hands in the process of righting herself. She knocked the plastic container out of Aldo's hand and onto the floor. As it landed, it splattered applesauce all around.

"Oh, no, Aldo," squeaked one of the girls nearby, remembering Mrs. Moss's words.

"Applesauce," shouted someone else. "Applesauce."

Aldo bent down to try and wipe up the mess with a napkin. His face and ears were red with embarrassment. All around him there were shouts and laughter.

"Aldo Sossi spilled his applesaucey."

"Applesauce. Applesauce."

And then, just as sure as his name was Aldo Sossi, Aldo knew that he had been given a nickname and he hated it: Applesauce.

CHAPTER FOUR

The First Weekend on Hillside La

Luckily for Aldo, the parent aides decided that it was too cold for the children to go outside after lunch. So everyone was herded into the auditorium, and they were shown some Popeye movies. DeDe said that she had seen the movies about 700 times already since she was in first grade. Every time it rained or snowed the children at the Woodside School were shown a Popeye movie instead of having outdoor recess, and the school owned only six different ones.

Aldo had never seen the films before, but he would have been willing just to sit in the darkened auditorium and do nothing. Anything would have been better than trying to join in at recess when everyone was calling him Applesauce. Today was Friday. Maybe by Monday morning they would have forgotten. Then he could start all over again.

Aldo had thought nothing else bad could happen that day. But it did. During the afternoon, he made the mistake of raising his hand to ask a question. Then when Mrs. Moss called on him, he accidentally mixed up her name with that of his old teacher, Miss Nesse, from P.S. 35 and said, "Mrs. Mess." The class hooted and howled with laughter. Mrs. Moss did not say anything in words, but Aldo had not liked the expression on her face. His own face once again turned a bright red, and he overheard someone at the next table whisper, "Look, his face is the color of applesauce." Of course, with all the commotion, Aldo forgot his question. No one was ever more delighted to hear a dismissal bell at three o'clock than Aldo was that day.

He rushed home passing Forest La, Maple La, and Cherry La until he reached Hillside. As he hurried inside the house, he realized that he had been in such a rush to get home that he hadn't thought about the trip. Luckily his legs had taken him in the right direction. His day had been awful, but it would have been even worse if he had gotten lost on the way home.

The weekend passed quickly. There was still lots of unpacking to be done. Aldo's parents were busy hanging pictures on the walls while Karen and Elaine unpacked books and dishes. After Aldo had arranged his new room to his satisfaction, he spent a lot of time watching Peabody and Poughkeepsie.

The cats had never before walked up and down stairs. Yet before the weekend was out they moved everywhere with agility. They found wonderful new hiding places throughout the house and in the basement. Aldo took them outdoors, one at a time. Poughkeepsie was always more cautious, and he stood on

the doorstep for a long time before he ventured into the front yard. There were little patches of snow remaining from the first fall of the winter, and he gingerly walked around them. When Peabody was permitted out, he was more venturesome. He sniffed at the snow and even tasted it. At the hardware store, Mr. Sossi bought collars for each cat with a place to write their name and their new address.

"Do you think they'll get lost?" Aldo worried. The cats had spent all their time in the old apartment and didn't know that life had more to offer.

"No," Mr. Sossi reassured his son. "We'll keep them in the house a bit longer till they know it well, and then if we let them out they'll be able to smell their way back home. They're going to like it here just as much as you and the girls."

Aldo wished there was a way of moving the new house back to their old neighborhood. Inside the house, Aldo loved it. From the window he could watch birds and squirrels in the trees. He was sure the yard would be full of discoveries for him in the springtime.

School was what made him unhappy. He didn't want to go back and be Applesauce again. There was no way of avoiding school, but he did forbid his mother to give him any of *that* to eat again.

"Aldo, you can't keep eliminating foods from your diet. First it was meat, then fish. Now you don't want applesauce. There won't be anything left to give you," she complained.

"I'll eat applesauce at home," promised Aldo. "It's just too messy to take to school."

On Monday Aldo returned to the Woodside School with reluctance and dread. But he didn't have any applesauce.

CHAPTER FIVE

A Fuss over Eggs

He did have an egg.

When Aldo took the items out of his lunch box on Monday, DeDe watched him carefully. He placed the hard-boiled egg on the table and reached for the cheese sandwich that was also in his box.

"No peanut butter today?" she asked. She was chewing away on a chopped-liver sandwich. It was on a big roll and it looked good, if you liked chopped liver.

Aldo moved his chair a couple of inches away from her so he wouldn't have to smell her

43

sandwich. "No peanut butter," he said, biting into his cheese.

"Hey, Applesauce, where's your sauce?" asked a boy at the next table. He wasn't even in Aldo's class, but the name had spread. In the morning when he arrived at school, a couple of boys had greeted him with the name. Aldo hoped the habit would wear off with time.

"Tell me about your dog," he asked DeDe, to change the subject.

"Well," said DeDe, removing her moustache, "I've had her for a year. And I'm teaching her tricks. I'm teaching her to cross only at green lights and not at red."

"I'm not sure," said Aldo, "but I think I read somewhere that dogs are color blind."

"Not Cookie," DeDe insisted.

Just then an arm reached between Aldo and DeDe and grabbed Aldo's egg. The arm tossed it to another boy. He tossed it to another, and the egg started making the rounds of the lunchroom. Aldo watched in amazement, wondering when the parent aides would stop the game.

"Whose egg is this?" one of the aides demanded. "Food is not to be played with, only eaten." She was a big woman and looked as if she ate lots of eggs and meat, and cakes and ice cream, too.

Aldo did not want to admit that the egg was his. Next they would be calling him Eggnog, he thought.

"Where did you get this egg?" the aide asked the last boy who had caught it. He grinned and pointed to the fellow who had thrown it to him.

"And where did you get it?" she asked him.

Obviously she wanted to track the egg back to its source. When she gets to me, I'll tell her I got it from a chicken, thought Aldo. But when the parent aide did reach him, he was too embarrassed. "It was in my lunch," was all he said.

"Then eat it!" she said, handing the egg to Aldo.

The shell was cracked and dirty from all the grubby hands that had held it since he had taken it out of his lunch box. Aldo didn't say anything, but he knew he wasn't going to be able to eat the egg. And he didn't think he would be able to bring another one in his lunch ever again either. What would his mother say about that!

"You think you're so funny!" said DeDe, turning to the boy who had first grabbed Aldo's egg. "Someday you'll get in big trouble."

"Oh, yeah? Who with—you?"

"Maybe," said DeDe, shrugging her shoulders and turning back to Aldo.

During social studies that afternoon, DeDe suddenly poked Aldo. Her moustache was back in place, but underneath it he could see her lips twitching into a smile. "Bring another egg tomorrow," she whispered.

"No," said Aldo.

"You must," she pleaded. "I've got a plan."

"Then you bring one, if you want it," said Aldo.

"You must," DeDe whispered urgently.

Aldo turned in his chair and pretended to be absorbed in the textbook in front of him. Why should he bring another hard-boiled egg to school and risk getting into trouble with it?

When school was over for the day, DeDe followed Aldo outside. "I have a great idea," she said, "but you must bring an egg tomorrow for it to work."

"Why don't *you* bring an egg?" said Aldo. "Why should I be the one?"

"I hate eggs. I haven't eaten one since I was a baby, so my mother would never cook one for me. But you could bring one without any problem."

"It's no problem for *you* if I bring an egg, just me," said Aldo. The thought crossed Aldo's mind that DeDe was the one who was responsible for knocking his container of applesauce onto the floor last week. If not for her, he wouldn't have gotten stuck with that stupid nickname. Now she was hatching a new scheme to mortify him using eggs.

"Trust me," said DeDe. "Aren't I your friend?"

Aldo looked at DeDe. He knew she hadn't meant to knock the applesauce down. It was an accident. He was glad that DeDe considered herself to be his friend.

"OK," he agreed. "I'll bring an egg tomorrow." Yet afterward, walking home toward Hillside Lane, Aldo felt he had consented too quickly. He should have said that he would bring an egg to school only on condition that she explain why she wore her silly moustache. Aldo was beginning to get used to it like the other kids in the class. But still he was curious about why she wore it.

At lunchtime the next day, DeDe reached eagerly for the egg that was in Aldo's lunch box next to his cream-cheese-and-jelly sandwich. She placed it conspicuously between them on the table.

"What's the matter with you?" asked Aldo. "Do you want someone to grab it again?"

"Yes!" DeDe grinned.

Sure enough, the boy at the next table again made a grab for the egg and threw it to one of his friends. The egg passed through at least half a dozen hands before the parent aide was able to stop them. This time she walked straight to where Aldo was sitting. "Is this your egg?" she asked, holding up the dirty, cracked oval.

"Yes, but I didn't throw it," said Aldo.

"Well, it sure didn't fly across the room," she said.

Somebody spilled something at another table, making a commotion and distracting her attention. Aldo turned to DeDe.

"See. I told you I would get into trouble."

"Don't worry," whispered DeDe. "I have a plan."

"Some plan," grumbled Aldo. "I don't want to be involved in your dumb plan."

She didn't say anything more. Even during

the afternoon, when they were working in committees on an art project and she could easily have spoken, DeDe said nothing. But when school let out, she followed closely behind Aldo.

"Bring another egg tomorrow," she said softly under her moustache.

"Never!" said Aldo.

"You must!" said DeDe.

"That's what you said yesterday," said Aldo, turning away from her. "Some friend you are!" Then he turned and ran off toward home.

Aldo worried about his mother giving him an egg in his lunch the next day, but he needn't have. She was not likely to give him eggs three days in a row. Even though she worried about his eating enough protein, she also worried about his eating too much cholesterol, which was something that was in eggs. So when Aldo sat down at the lunch table, he had only a peanut-butter sandwich and a carrot in his lunch box.

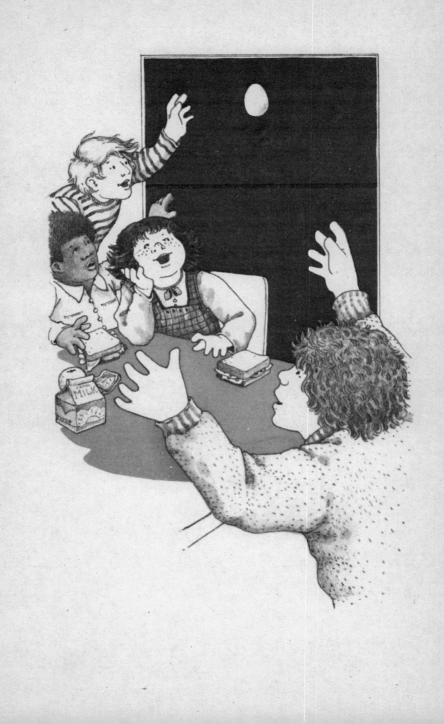

Aldo had not wanted to sit next to DeDe today, but there was no other vacant seat. He bit into his carrot and didn't say anything as she removed her food from her box.

To Aldo's surprise, she removed an egg, which was wrapped in a napkin, and placed it on the table between them.

"I thought you didn't like eggs," said Aldo.

"I don't," said DeDe, removing her moustache and biting into a sardine sandwich.

"Then why did you bring it?" Aldo started to ask.

But before he had finished his question, a hand reached between them and grabbed the egg and threw it across the room. Aldo watched as another boy held out his hand to make the catch. The egg smashed in his hand, oozing all over his shirt sleeve. It was raw!

Aldo looked at DeDe. She was calmly chewing on her sandwich as if nothing had happened. All around them children were shouting and laughing, but DeDe was acting as if raw eggs flew through the air every day.

The parent aide marched over to Aldo.

"Was that your idea of a joke?" she asked.

"No," said Aldo honestly. He was about to say that he hadn't even brought the egg to school, but he didn't want to tell on DeDe.

"I don't play with food," he said.

"I don't think anyone else will after this either," said the aide. For the first time she smiled at Aldo. "That was a good trick. He deserved it," she said, as she walked off.

Aldo looked at DeDe. She was putting her moustache back on as she always did after lunch. Even though it hid most of her mouth, he could see that she was smiling at him.

"I told you I couldn't bring a hard-boiled egg," she said. "So I brought a raw one."

CHAPTER SIX

Fussing over the Birds

On Friday evening there was a special on TV, and Aldo's parents let him stay up until almost midnight. The next morning it was gray and bitter cold outside. Aldo snuggled under the covers in his new bedroom and slept later than he had ever slept before.

It was 11:30 when he finally got out of bed, and it was noon before he was dressed and had brushed his teeth. He went into the kitchen to fix himself something to eat. He found an open box of cold cereal on the table and poured some into a bowl. He cut up a banana on top and added milk. Just as he was finishing the cereal Karen and his mother walked into the kitchen with brown grocery bags in their arms.

"If you're finished eating, you can help us unload the car," said Mrs. Sossi. "We bought enough food to feed an army, but in this house I'll be lucky if it lasts a week."

Aldo reached for some bread and put two slices in the toaster. "What are you doing?" asked his mother. "Didn't you just eat?"

"That was breakfast," Aldo explained. "Now I'm fixing some lunch."

Karen giggled and went outside to get another bag of groceries from the car. "On second thought," said Mrs. Sossi, "maybe this food will only last over the weekend."

Lunch for Aldo consisted of two slices of toast and two slices of American cheese and a glass of orange juice.

"Why don't you eat the crusts?" asked Mrs. Sossi. "Don't tell me you aren't hungry!"

"I didn't want them," said Aldo, "and besides, I want to feed them to the birds." He took the crusts from his plate and also the end slices of bread, which always got left in the bag anyhow, and broke them into little pieces. Then he opened the back door by the kitchen and threw the crumbs out into the yard. Peabody came and stood by the door looking out, but he stayed in the warm house.

After he closed the door, Aldo stood by the kitchen window and began counting. He had discovered that somewhere between the count of seventy and one hundred the birds would arrive when he put food out. First one came timidly hopping close to the offering, and then suddenly a dozen others appeared, all pushing and grabbing like his classmates on the lunch line. Aldo was fascinated by the birds and thought he could watch them all day long.

"Is there anything else we could give the birds?" Aldo asked. Then he remembered. "Did you buy some bird seed for the feeder?"

"They only had ten-pound bags," said Mrs. Sossi, "and I had enough things to buy as it was. Maybe next week," she said, seeing her son's disappointed face.

"Well, can I throw out more bread?" begged Aldo.

"Enough is enough," argued Mrs. Sossi. "I have to worry about feeding our family and the cats. I can't assume responsibility for all the birds in the neighborhood too."

Aldo looked in the refrigerator and found a dish containing some leftover spaghetti from three nights before. "Is anyone going to eat this?" he asked.

"I doubt it," said his mother.

"Then I'll give it to the birds," said Aldo triumphantly. "They'll think it's a new kind of worm."

"Aldo is trying to make vegetarians out of the sparrows," Mrs. Sossi observed to her husband as he walked into the kitchen.

Sure enough, within minutes the sparrows, joined by some starlings and a blue jay, were fighting over the spaghetti strands. Aldo didn't

58

know if they actually thought they were eating worms or not. It didn't matter. He had once read that a bird must eat an amount equal to its weight every day to stay alive. They had to work hard in the winter when the ground was frozen over, and Aldo was proud to be able to help them out.

"Oh, look at this!" wailed Mrs. Sossi. "Someone put this jar of wheat germ in the cupboard when we moved. It's supposed to be refrigerated or it loses its food value." Ever since Aldo had become a vegetarian, his mother had been supplementing his diet with health foods like wheat germ and milkshakes made with yeast and honey and lecithin.

"I guess we better throw it out and get a fresh jar," she said, taking the wheat germ and throwing it into the garbage.

Aldo had quick reflexes. If wheat germ was good for him, it would probably be good for the birds too. Even if it hadn't been refrigerated, at least it would help them get their day's quota of food. He took the jar from the garbage pail, and for the third time in the past half hour he went out the back door. Carefully he sprinkled the wheat germ under the old maple tree.

"We'll have the toughest, strongest birds in the neighborhood," Mr. Sossi said with a laugh. "I wonder how they ever managed before we moved here."

Elaine came walking into the kitchen with her new friend, Sandy.

"*J'ai faim,*" she said.

"*Moi aussi,*" said Sandy. She was also studying French.

Just to be sure that everyone understood, Elaine added a few words in English. "We're starved. What's left for people to eat?" she asked. "I bet *your* family doesn't throw all their food out the window," she said to Sandy.

Aldo thought of correcting her. He hadn't thrown anything out the window. He had taken it out the back door. He decided not to make the effort. Elaine just wouldn't under-

stand why he cared about the birds. Instead, he counted them. There were fourteen, all eating at once, and two squirrels had joined them too.

"The next time you go shopping," Aldo said, turning to his mother, "I think you should buy some nuts. They're good for vegetarians like me," he said. But he was thinking about the squirrels.

CHAPTER SEVEN

Settling In

By the end of the first few weeks, all the Sossi family seemed to be settling into their new life on Hillside Lane. Elaine had quickly made friends with Sandy, who conveniently lived only three houses away. They were both in the ninth grade, and in addition to showing off their newly acquired French vocabulary, they also shared other interests: boys, clothes, and rock music.

Karen hadn't made a close friend yet, but she kept busy sending letters to her old friends in the city. Her English teacher had a list of pen pals, and Karen had started corresponding with a boy named Keichi in Japan and a girl named Iris in England. Elaine had instructed Karen to be on the lookout for a French boy that she could write to also. When Karen's first letter from Japan arrived, she was more excited than Aldo had seen her in months. After running around to show it to everyone, she sat down immediately to answer it. She kept very busy writing letters to friends she never saw anymore or friends she might never meet. Unless, of course, the Sossi family went to Japan for their summer vacation, which seemed highly unlikely.

Mrs. Sossi was busy fixing up the new house. She had registered for two courses in the local adult-education program. One was in carpentry and the other in plumbing. She was building some new shelves for Aldo's room, but luckily she hadn't needed to try out her plumbing skills so far. Still, everyone warned that toilets stopped up and bathtubs overflowed frequently in old houses, and she was determined to be prepared.

Mr. Sossi was preoccupied with his new job. Actually, he was working for the same company, but he had been transferred to another division in another location, and so the job seemed like a new one. On weekends he walked about the house planning future projects like building on a screened porch and making a brick patio in the back. But he didn't have time to do anything more than just think about these ideas now, and besides, he explained to everyone, the winter was not a good time for building.

Aldo, too, was settling in. Slowly.

At school he was still called Applesauce. Some days he winced when he walked into the school yard and he heard someone shout, "Here comes Applesauce!"

Other days he pretended that he didn't hear anything at all. He had learned the names of all the children in his class. He had grown to like Mrs. Moss, and he hadn't made the mistake of calling her Mrs. Mess again. Studying the planets was fun. He had gone to the

Hayden planetarium in New York on a chartered bus with his new class, and it was very interesting. Aldo wondered if there were animals living on any other planets. Maybe just tiny animals like insects.

The fourth grade was also studying the metric system, and in the afternoons Mrs. Moss read aloud from a book about a boy who called his brother The Great Brain. If it wasn't for the applesauce business, Aldo would have enjoyed school.

One Friday afternoon, a boy named Scott asked Aldo if he ever went bowling. When Aldo said that he never had, Scott looked pleased. "Why don't you come with me tomorrow?" he invited.

They arranged to meet in front of the school at eleven the next morning and walk to the bowling alley together. Mr. Sossi was so pleased that Aldo was making a new friend that he cheerfully gave him the necessary money for playing. Bowling was rather silly, Aldo decided at the bowling alley the next day. You had to put on special sneakers that you rented from the bowling alley, even if you were already wearing your own sneakers. They cost thirty-five cents. Then you had to try and roll a heavy ball and hit the pins. Aldo hit a few. A very few. His total score for the first game was thirty. Scott had obviously played often because he hit many more pins and his score was seventy-five. They played a second game, but Aldo's heart wasn't in it. Scott said he wanted to become a champion bowler. He had an older brother on the high-school bowling team, and he wanted to be on the team when he got to high school too, so he came as often as he could to practice.

Aldo was glad when the game was over. He was glad, too, that there wasn't enough money for another game. The boys walked back in the direction of the school. For some reason, Aldo couldn't think of anything to say. Scott kept talking about his old bowling scores. "The worst I ever got was forty-five," he said, "and I was only in second grade then. Once

I got ninety. That's very good for a kid my size."

Aldo nodded. "Say," he asked Scott, "do you know why DeDe wears that fake moustache?" The question kept worrying Aldo. Maybe now he would finally get an answer.

Scott shrugged his shoulders. "Oh, she's just crazy," he said. "She's been in my class since kindergarten. She always does things to show off or to be different. You'll get used to her."

Aldo nodded again.

"Do you want to come bowling with me next week?" Scott asked. "You'll probably get better at it if you do it some more."

"Thanks," said Aldo. "But I think I'm going to be busy."

"Well, OK, Applesauce," said Scott. "See you in school on Monday." The two boys went in opposite directions.

As he walked, Aldo thought about DeDe. Maybe the reason he was curious about her was because she was different, as Scott had said. She seemed more interesting than any of the other kids in his class. He bet she wouldn't waste time doing something as silly as bowling. He wondered what she was doing today instead.

Aldo returned home to Peabody and Poughkeepsie. They were settling in at Hillside Lane too. He liked to know that they were always waiting for him, just like the old days. Sometimes one or both of the cats would be walking about the yard or sitting on the doorstep. They always walked over to Aldo and then rubbed slowly against his legs when he approached. They were truly his best friends. Maybe someday he would invite DeDe over to meet them. He thought they would like her. They would think her moustache was a kind of whiskers.

CHAPTER EIGHT

The Birthday Party

Aldo seldom received any mail. So he was surprised to come home from school one day and find an envelope addressed to him.

"Pouks," he asked Poughkeepsie, who was standing nearby, "who is writing to me?" Inside the envelope was an invitation to a birthday party on Saturday afternoon. The party was for Frank Rudolph, who was in his class. Aldo tried to remember if he had ever said anything to Frank or if Frank had ever said anything to him. As far as he could remember, the two of them had not exchanged a single word during the two months that Aldo had

73

been in his new fourth-grade class. Maybe Frank wanted to be his friend. Maybe he liked him very much even though Aldo hadn't noticed any special friendliness yet.

So the next morning in school, Aldo walked up to Frank and said, "I got your invitation. I'm coming to your party on Saturday." Then he asked, "How did you know my address?" He was curious about the details of this new friendship.

"Oh, my mother gets a list from the school. I always invite all the boys in my class every year. The more kids, the more presents," Frank said, grinning.

Aldo tried to smile back. Apparently Frank didn't think of him as a friend after all.

Somebody said, "Hey, Red! I got your invitation." Frank grinned again. Even though he had black hair, most of the boys called him Red. Aldo decided he would have to ask DeDe about the nickname. Maybe his hair had been red when he was little.

On Saturday, Aldo's father drove him to

Frank's house. "He's called Red," Aldo explained to his father. "It's because his last name is Rudolph and so his nickname is 'Rudolph the Red-Nosed Reindeer.' Almost everyone calls him Red except the teacher," said Aldo. He kept talking as if Frank Rudolph was a good friend. Aldo knew his father was eager for him to make new friends, and also Aldo was trying to convince himself that he wanted to be going to this party. It was a lunch party, and he was nervous about what kind of food they would serve.

Mr. Sossi started to laugh. "I guess kids haven't changed very much," he said.

"What do you mean?" asked Aldo.

"Oh, I was just thinking of some of the nicknames kids had when I was at school."

"Did you have a nickname?" asked Aldo.

"Not me, but your uncle Tom sure did."

The car stopped in front of a red-brick house. "This is the number," said Mr. Sossi. "Look, that must be one of the guests going to the party."

Aldo saw another boy from his class walking toward the front steps of the house, and so he quickly opened the car door. Entering a strange house with someone else was easier than going in alone.

"Have a good time," his father called. "I'll be back for you at three when the party is over."

"Hi, Michael," Aldo shouted.

The door opened even before they rang the bell. Half the school seemed to be inside, but of course there weren't that many at all. Red sat on the floor surrounded by a pile of packages, one bigger than another. Aldo was afraid his present looked very small when he gave it to him to add to the pile. It was a model-airplane kit, which his father had helped him to pick out in a shop on the way to the party.

Soon Mrs. Rudolph told all the boys to come into the dining room for lunch. Aldo worried again about what they would be having to eat. His mother had told him just to say "no thank you," if he was offered anything that he wouldn't eat. Most days it wasn't so hard to be a vegetarian, but Aldo had a feeling that this day was going to be a hard one.

There were fifteen boys sitting around the table. Most of them Aldo recognized from school, but there were a couple of others whom he didn't know. He took a seat between Michael and Scott.

Maybe we'll have pizza, he thought. Lots of times people served pizza at birthday parties.

Mr. and Mrs. Rudolph walked into the dining room, each holding a large platter. "We have hot dogs and hamburgers," said Mr. Rudolph. "And there's enough for everyone to have one of each."

Aldo's stomach flipped. He should have stayed home. He couldn't eat hot dogs *or* hamburgers. When he had first become a vegetarian he was sometimes tempted to eat meat. But with the passing of many months, his tastes had changed. Meat no longer tempted

77

him at all. Red's father walked around the table, putting a hamburger in a bun on each plate. Red's mother walked around the table putting some chips on each plate. At least Aldo could eat them. He tried to look as if he were eating like the other boys. He drank some of the orange soda in his paper cup and pushed the chips around on his plate. A dish of pickles was passed down the table, and Aldo took one.

"Finish up, boys, and I'll give you the hot dogs," said Mrs. Rudolph.

Aldo had an idea. He turned to Scott, who was sitting on his left. "Would you like my hamburger?" he asked. "I'm not so hungry."

"No," said Scott. "I want to save plenty of room for the cake and ice cream."

Aldo noticed that some of the boys left part of their buns on their plates. Maybe no one would notice that he hadn't touched his at all.

Mr. Rudolph started distributing hot dogs. "Here's one for you," he said to Aldo. "You're a very slow eater."

"No, thank you," said Aldo. "I'm not very hungry."

"He only eats applesauce," said Michael. Everyone laughed, and Aldo felt his ears and face growing red.

"That's Aldo Applesauce," said Red to his father. "He's new."

"Where do you come from, Aldo?" asked Mr. Rudolph. "Don't boys eat hot dogs where you come from?"

"I used to live in New York City," said Aldo. "But I'm a vegetarian. I don't like animals to be killed, so I just don't eat any meat."

"Boy, you are crazy!" said Michael. "No wonder you eat so much applesauce."

"And eggs," added another boy at the end of the table.

All the boys but Aldo laughed again.

"I bet *he* eats vegetables," said Mrs. Rudolph to her son. "Frank thinks the world would come to an end if he had to eat a carrot," she said to Aldo.

Aldo wished he was sitting anywhere except at Red's dining-room table. He would rather have been at school or in a doctor's waiting room or in the dentist's chair. Anywhere would have been better than here where he was the center of attention and everyone was calling him Applesauce and laughing at him.

When the cake was served, Mrs. Rudolph gave him an extra large slice because she was worried that he would go home hungry. Aldo's stomach was still flipping about from the business over the hamburgers and the hot dogs, so he wasn't even hungry for cake with blue-and-green frosting and little plastic baseball players. Luckily, Scott leaned over to Aldo and offered to help him finish the cake. Aldo gave it and also the ice cream to him. He had no appetite whatsoever.

After the eating came the opening of the presents. Red tore the wrappers off all the gifts so quickly that Aldo couldn't keep track of who gave him what. The gift cards quickly got mixed up, and ten minutes after he opened

the presents, Frank Rudolph no longer knew or cared who gave him what. Aldo was relieved to see that he had received another model kit—for a submarine. At least no one could say his was a stupid present.

The rest of the party was spent in the dark. Mr. Rudolph had rented a motion-picture projector, and he showed the old version of *King Kong,* which he had also rented. Everyone had seen the film on TV, but no one objected to seeing it again.

"Now you know why I couldn't invite any girls," said Red. "They would be screaming every time they saw the gorilla."

Aldo was glad that King Kong was a man dressed up as a gorilla and not a real animal being used in the film. The mention of the girls in his class made him think of DeDe. He wondered what she was doing today. He would have preferred being with her, he thought, instead of being here. Fortunately, he was now sitting on the floor in the dark, one of many boys and not being singled out. Soon the party would be over, and his father would take him home.

"Move over, Applesauce," said one of the boys. "I can't see."

By the time both reels of the film were finished and the party was over, Aldo's stomach, which had not permitted him to eat anything before, began to protest that it was empty. Luckily, the projector had made so much noise that no one could hear the grumbling coming from Aldo's stomach. At three there was a scramble of boys rushing off to the cars waiting for them outside. Aldo quietly made his departure. Happily, his father was parked at the curb outside waiting for him.

"Dad," said Aldo, before his father could ask him about the party, "you didn't tell me what name Uncle Tom had when he was a boy."

"What?" asked Mr. Sossi.

"You know. You said he had a nickname," Aldo reminded his father.

Whatever it was, thought Aldo, it couldn't be as bad as Applesauce.

Mr. Sossi started to laugh. "I hadn't thought about it in years," he said. "And I was lucky to have escaped. Do you want to make a guess?"

Aldo Sossi, alias Applesauce, shook his head. He had no ideas. There was nothing, he thought, that could compare with Applesauce.

"Well," said his father, "with a name like Thomas Sossi, I suppose it was inevitable. They called him Tomato Sauce."

CHAPTER NINE

The Phone Number

Ever since the incident with the raw egg in the lunchroom, Aldo felt a close bond with DeDe. They never again mentioned the business of the eggs, but it was like an unspoken secret between them. Yet when Aldo hesitantly asked DeDe what she did on the weekends, hoping that she would invite him to come and see her dog Cookie, she said, "My father usually takes me someplace special."

Sure enough, the next Friday afternoon when Aldo asked her what she was doing on Saturday, DeDe said, "My father is taking me to Pennsylvania."

And so the weeks passed, and although they sat side by side in the classroom and in the lunchroom, Aldo didn't really know DeDe any better than before. She was often preoccupied, and sometimes she seemed quite sad. Aldo felt bad that she was unhappy, but he didn't know what to do about it. He still didn't know why she wore her moustache. Everyone else in the class seemed to ignore the existence of it, and for the most part they seemed to ignore DeDe too. Aldo tried to do the first, but he didn't even attempt to do the second. He really wanted DeDe to be his friend.

One Friday at lunchtime, Aldo noticed that DeDe seemed to be especially glum. She hardly ate any of her lunch, and she didn't respond to any of Aldo's conversation. He was telling her about how Peabody had jumped into the open washing machine when it was half filled with dirty clothing. Then when Mrs. Sossi returned with more laundry, she threw it on top of the other things in the machine. Next

she sprinkled soap powder on top of everything, and Peabody came leaping out of the
machine, startling Aldo's mother. The cat
gave a series of sneezes, obviously caused by
the soap in his nose. It was a funny story,
especially since it had a happy ending and the
cat hadn't gotten locked into a machine full
of water. But DeDe hardly seemed to listen.

During the recess period after lunch, Aldo
left her and went to join a soccer baseball
game with some of the others. He kept thinking about DeDe. He wondered what was
bothering her.

"Hey, Applesauce! Kick the ball over here,"
shouted Red.

Aldo was jolted out of his thoughts. He still
hadn't gotten used to that nickname, and he
kicked the ball with anger.

During the afternoon, DeDe sat at her place
not paying any attention to the classwork. At
dismissal time, however, she followed Aldo
outside and startled him by asking, "What
are you doing tomorrow?"

"Nothing," said Aldo. "Do you want to come over to my house to play? You can see my cats."

"Why not?" DeDe shrugged halfheartedly.

She took a pen out of her book bag and grabbed Aldo's hand. "Here's my number," she said, writing her phone number on the back of his hand.

"Call me tonight, and we'll decide what time I should come."

"Sure," said Aldo.

He was pleased that he would finally get to know DeDe a little better. It was cold so he took his mittens out of his jacket pocket and put them on, stopping for a moment to admire the phone number temporarily tattooed on his hand. He would call DeDe right after supper.

When Aldo got home, his mother reminded him to clean out the cats' litter pan first thing. After he finished, he washed his hands and came into the kitchen looking for a snack.

His mother gave him an apple and then asked him to help peel the potatoes for supper.

Aldo was in such a good mood thinking about DeDe coming over the next day that he didn't even protest about this additional chore. He peeled the potatoes and rinsed them off carefully. He even washed up around the sink without having to be asked.

That evening after supper, Aldo rushed to the telephone. "I have to make a call," he announced to his family.

He looked at the back of his hand to read the number.

But his hands had been washed at least four times since he had come home from school, and the numbers had become a blur.

"Comment allez-vous?" asked Elaine, coming upon Aldo in the hallway. Aldo was not in the mood for listening to Elaine show off her new French words.

"Speak English!" he said. "I was supposed to call someone from school, but the numbers got washed away." He held up his smudged hand.

"There is an invention called paper," said Elaine. "Even a kid in fourth grade should have heard of that." But as she spoke, she reached for the phone book. "Here, I'll help you look up the number. What's the last name?"

"Rawson," said Aldo.

There was no one listed named Rawson.

"There are two possibilities," said Elaine. "Either it is a new listing, like ours, and isn't in the phone book yet, or it is an unlisted number, and then the operator won't tell it to you."

"Could you call the operator for me?" begged Aldo. He was feeling worse and worse about the blurred figures on his hand. He wished he could read them.

Elaine dialed the operator. Within a moment she was able to report to Aldo that there was no listing for Rawson. "Maybe your friend doesn't really have a telephone number at all," she said.

Aldo shook his head. DeDe might enjoy jokes sometimes, like the business with the raw egg and wearing a fake moustache, but he was sure she wanted him to call her. He wondered what he would do the next day. And he wondered what DeDe would think when he didn't phone her. Probably she would decide that he didn't want to be her friend after all.

"Oh, well," said Elaine. *"C'est dommage."*

Aldo didn't know what the words meant. And he didn't care.

CHAPTER TEN

Aldo Takes a Walk

The next morning Aldo was very restless. He was sure DeDe would be angry because he hadn't phoned her. Now they would never become friends. He didn't feel like playing any of his games, or watching TV, or reading a book. He didn't even feel like playing with Peabody and Poughkeepsie. Usually, when everything else failed him, the cats came through. He loved watching them or playing games with them. But today he wanted to play with a person.

Elaine had a date with her friend Sandy. And Karen was busy reading a cookbook. At school she was taking a course called Teen Action. It was a fancy name for cooking, and although Karen had never shown any particular interest in the affairs of the kitchen, except at mealtime, she had signed up for it when she entered her new school. The wonder of the Teen Action course was that, after a few weeks, Karen had become fascinated with cooking and now she read cookbooks the way other people read mysteries.

Sometimes in the evening she would look up from the book she was reading and sigh, "That was delicious!" Usually it was a recipe for something like chocolate mousse or oatmeal-raisin-nut cookies.

"Here's a good recipe," she said now, showing a page to her mother.

"You could make that, if you want," said Mrs. Sossi. "It looks interesting and not too hard. I don't have any dessert in the house for the weekend. Only I don't have any applesauce." She looked at Aldo walking restlessly about. "Aldo! How about running up to the supermarket and buying a jar of applesauce so Karen can make this cake for all of us?''

Aldo winced at the word *applesauce*. But he could not think of any excuse to stay home, and so he took the dollar that his mother handed him and put on his winter jacket.

Now that it was March, he could see signs of the beginnings of spring. Little crocus flowers were poking up out of the ground, and there seemed to be more birds about than ever. Walking along, Aldo watched two squirrels chase one another up a tree and along some high branches. They looked like a pair of friends playing tag. It must be fun to be a squirrel, Aldo thought. He had some money in his pants pocket because he had gotten his allowance that morning, and he decided that he would buy a bag of peanuts to feed the squirrels on his way home.

At the supermarket, he took a jar of applesauce off the shelf and stood on the express line. He looked about anxiously. It would be dreadful if he met someone from school. He could just imagine the teasing. "Applesauce buying applesauce."

He felt better when the jar was safely hidden in a brown paper bag. Next door to the supermarket was a candy store, and Aldo remembered seeing small cellophane bags of peanuts at the candy counter. There was also a revolving rack with small toys and novelties. Aldo stood turning it and looking at the various items. He saw a trick nickel that could squirt water, rubber spiders, and a piece of plastic that looked like a slice of cheese. Then he saw some packages with fake moustaches. They must have been left over from Halloween. He wondered if DeDe had bought her moustache here. The package cost twenty-five cents, and Aldo decided to buy one. He put the peanuts in his pocket and rested the bag with the applesauce on the counter for a minute while he put on his moustache. Then he picked up his bag and started out the candy store. Just as he emerged on the street he saw

DeDe standing by the curb. She was wearing her moustache.

"Hi," Aldo said, grinning at her from underneath his moustache. "I bought one too."

"It isn't funny," said DeDe.

"Who says you're the only one who can wear a moustache?" demanded Aldo.

"Why didn't you call me? You said you would," DeDe asked, pulling her moustache off and putting it in her pocket.

"I know," said Aldo. "But I washed my hands and your number came off."

"Which way are you going?" DeDe asked, walking with Aldo.

"I'm going home. I have to bring this," he said, and he held up the paper bag.

"What's inside?" DeDe asked.

"I'll tell you if you don't laugh," Aldo said. DeDe nodded in agreement.

"Applesauce."

DeDe started laughing.

Aldo was angry. "You said you wouldn't

laugh," he protested. "How come you wear that moustache all the time? Girls don't wear moustaches."

"So what!" said DeDe. "It's my business. I can do what I want."

They walked along the street without speaking. Then DeDe said, "Are you going home to eat your applesauce?"

"No. My sister is going to use it to bake a cake," said Aldo. He waited a minute. Then he said, "Would you like to come and watch? You could see Peabody and Poughkeepsie, too."

"OK," said DeDe. "I don't have anything special to do today anyhow." She paused a moment before she spoke again. "Does your father have a moustache?"

Aldo removed his and smiled at DeDe. "Nobody at my house has a moustache except the cats. They have whiskers."

CHAPTER ELEVEN

Applesauce Cake

Karen was waiting to make her cake. It was a chocolate applesauce cake. She said that Aldo and DeDe could watch if they didn't get in the way and if they were quiet. Karen needed quiet to concentrate when she was cooking. Aldo and DeDe sat on chairs around the kitchen table and watched as Karen prepared to create a work of art from the written recipe.

Karen assembled the ingredients: cooking oil, baking chocolate, sugar, eggs, flour, nuts, raisins, cinnamon, and, of course, applesauce. Aldo enjoyed watching because none of the preparations involved meat or fish. Although he was a vegetarian, he had not yet persuaded anyone else in his family to abandon the eating of animals. Happily, he could and did eat cakes and pies with a clean conscience.

The batter was very stiff, and Karen seemed to be having difficulty stirring it.

"Can we have a piece when it's finished?" Aldo asked.

Karen greased the baking pan as she had been taught at school. Then she poured the batter into it and put the pan in the oven. "The cake should be ready in forty-five minutes," she said, smiling proudly. "Then you can both have a piece."

Aldo and DeDe went to find Peabody and Poughkeepsie. They sat on the living-room rug, and each of them stroked one of the cats. Before long the aroma of the baking cake began to fill the house. It was a wonderful apple-cinnamon-chocolate smell.

"I guess applesauce is OK in a cake," said Aldo. "But I sure hate it for a name."

"You do?" asked DeDe. "You're a dodo. It's great. Lots of kids would be glad to have that nickname. It makes you special."

"What do you mean?" asked Aldo.

"Some kids have nicknames and some don't," explained DeDe. "My real name is Denise Diane, but no one calls me that. Then Louis Roberts is called Louisiana, and Michael Frank is called Frankfurter, but Frank Rudolph is called Red. Lorraine Gibbons is called the Ape. We used to have a boy in our class named Peter Underwood. Everyone called him Underwear, but he moved away last year. Everybody in the school knows you better if you have a nickname. It's sort of like being famous."

"Maybe you're right," said Aldo thoughtfully. "Even some of the boys in the sixth grade say hello to me. A nickname isn't so bad, but I wish I had a different one."

"It's not something you can choose," DeDe pointed out.

"I have an uncle named Thomas Sossi. He

was called Tomato Sauce when he was my age," said Aldo. "I guess it's my fate."

"It's like a tradition," said DeDe. "You'll get used to it. And besides, it could be worse."

"Yeah. I would hate to be called Underwear," said Aldo. He was beginning to feel a little better about his name. When DeDe called him Applesauce, it sounded friendly, not teasing.

They went into the kitchen to watch Karen take the cake from the oven. Some of the batter had risen above the top of the pan. Some of it had dropped out onto the bottom of the oven. The top of the cake was all burned and black looking.

"I must have used too much applesauce," said Karen with disgust. "I thought the batter was too thick, so I finished up the whole jar. I hate applesauce," she said, looking at her burned and lopsided cake. "Look what it did to my cake!" She started crying.

"Don't worry," Mrs. Sossi said, trying to console her daughter. "We can slice off the

burned section of the cake and eat the rest of it. All cooks have failures sometimes."

But when the cake had cooled and it was cut, they discovered that the middle of it was still uncooked and soggy. The whole thing was fit only for the garbage.

"No, wait," said Aldo, grabbing up the cake as Karen was about to deposit it into the trash can.

He took the cake outside and set it under the maple tree. Then he stood by the window with DeDe, watching. For a long time nothing happened. Then suddenly a squirrel ran down the trunk of the tree and stopped to sniff the unusual-looking object at the tree's base. He nibbled at it before running off again. Perhaps he went to tell his friends, thought Aldo. Before long the yard was filled with birds and squirrels that were all feasting away.

Aldo called Karen to come and see the success of her cake. "When do you think you'll bake another one?" Aldo asked her.

"Not today," she said with a sigh, her eyes

red. Still, she was already holding a new cookbook and beginning to study it.

"Please make another one soon," Aldo begged. It was nice to think that whether the cake succeeded or failed it would still be enjoyed. "I could buy some more applesauce if you want," he offered.

"It seems to me," said Mrs. Sossi, looking out the window at the busy creatures in her backyard, "that if I were a squirrel in this neighborhood, I'd hurry and open a branch of Weight Watchers. Soon we're going to have the most enormous squirrels in town. And the birds will be too fat to fly."

DeDe spent the rest of the day visiting at Aldo's house. Aldo carefully wrote down her phone number on a piece of paper and pinned it on his bulletin board. He wasn't going to risk losing it a second time.

In the late afternoon, he walked DeDe partway home. Aldo felt the moustache and the bag of peanuts in his jacket pocket where he had left them in the morning. He decided to

110

save the peanuts to feed the squirrels another day when they hadn't been served a burned cake for their lunch.

As for the moustache, he guessed he wouldn't wear it again unless he needed it for a part in a school play or maybe for dressing up next Halloween.

CHAPTER TWELVE

At DeDe's House

Aldo looked forward to visiting at DeDe's house the next Saturday. In the first place, she already knew he was a vegetarian and so she wouldn't embarrass him by serving a piece of some animal or other at lunchtime. In the second place, he loved dogs and he was eager to meet DeDe's dog Cookie. But most of all, he was glad that after all these weeks he and DeDe were becoming friends at last.

Aldo did have some questions in his mind. He always wondered about the business with the moustache. Maybe it was a family thing, and her mother wore a fake moustache too.

112

Maybe she belonged to some special religion that required moustaches, the way Daniel Levy in his old class used to wear a little round cap to cover the top of his head. By visiting at DeDe's house, Aldo hoped to discover the answer to his question at last.

When he put on his jacket on Saturday morning, he found the moustache that he had bought the week before still in his pocket. He wondered why DeDe had gotten so angry when she saw him wearing it. Maybe she thought he was making fun of her.

His house was only four short blocks from DeDe's house. He was glad because he didn't need to depend on either of his parents to drive him in the car. He rang the bell, and the door was opened immediately. DeDe must have been standing inside it just waiting for him to come. She was not wearing her moustache this morning.

DeDe's mother was not wearing a moustache either. She had blond hair and blue eyes, unlike DeDe, who had dark brown hair and eyes. Aldo decided that if he had seen her in a room full of parents he would not have matched her up with DeDe. Some kids were just small-sized versions of their parents.

Cookie jumped all over Aldo. She was a friendly dog and liked to smell new people all over. Aldo laughed to see Cookie's excitement. Poughkeepsie and Peabody greeted newcomers very differently. First they would ignore the person, and then eventually they would walk past them and perhaps even sniff at them. To Aldo their manner seemed to say, "We know enough people already. You aren't very important to us." Cookie, on the other hand, seemed to be saying, "I like you and I want you to be my friend."

Cookie knew several tricks. She would fetch a ball if Aldo or DeDe threw it across the room. She could shake hands (paws, actually), and she would roll over at DeDe's command.

But when it was lunchtime, DeDe locked Cookie up in the basement.

"Why are you doing that?" Aldo asked.

"We have to, or else she drives us crazy with her begging. You'd think we never fed her at all," said DeDe. "She comes to the table and whines and whines."

"Or else she puts her head right into your lap while you're eating," said DeDe's mother.

Mrs. Rawson served plates of spaghetti to the children. Aldo could see that DeDe had told her mother about him. There were no meatballs in the sauce. Aldo reached for his plate as Mrs. Rawson slid it to him across the counter. The side of the plate was unexpectedly hot, and Aldo instinctively let go. As he did so, the plate tipped and all the spaghetti and sauce went sliding off his plate and onto the floor.

"Oh," he gasped. "I'm sorry." He stood helplessly looking at the mess.

"Is it OK, Mom?" DeDe asked.

Her mother nodded. "Cheer up, Aldo. This isn't the first time something has spilled in this house, and it won't be the last."

As she spoke, DeDe ran to open the base-

ment door. Instantly, Cookie was leaping into
the room. With a single motion, the dog
gulped up the food from the floor. And within
seconds, no one could have said where the
spaghetti had fallen.

"She's a super vacuum cleaner," said DeDe,
grinning. "It's probably her best trick of all."

Aldo's plate was refilled while Cookie was
returned to the basement. He sat with DeDe
and her mother eating his lunch.

"You should have seen Cookie last summer
when we stayed at a motel by Echo Lake in
Vermont," said DeDe. "We went into our
room, and Cookie ran all over exploring it.
Then we heard her growling from under the
bed. We looked under the bed and saw that
she had some furry animal in her mouth."

"Oh, did she kill it?" asked Aldo, feeling
upset. He understood that animals were often
killed in nature, but still the thought always
made him feel unhappy.

"No," DeDe said, laughing. "It wasn't an

animal. It was a wig that had been left by the people who stayed in the room before us."

"I guess you could say she killed the wig. It certainly wasn't fit to be worn again after Cookie got through with it." Mrs. Rawson laughed.

"My father took a great picture of her with the wig still in her mouth," said DeDe. She had begun the sentence still laughing, but somewhere in the middle of it her voice changed and grew sad.

"Could I see it?" asked Aldo. "It sounds really funny."

"Yes," said DeDe, but without any enthusiasm.

When lunch was over, Cookie was once again released from the basement. The children took her for a long walk, and Aldo enjoyed having a turn holding the leash. He pretended she was his dog, and he decided that he would increase his efforts to convince his parents that the Sossi family needed a dog.

He was sure that Peabody and Poughkeepsie could also learn to like a dog.

Back in the house, Aldo again asked DeDe about the photograph of Cookie with the wig. DeDe took out an album and showed Aldo. Across the page from the picture of Cookie was a man who strongly resembled DeDe.

"Is this your father?" he asked. The man had the same dark hair and eyes as DeDe.

"Yes," said DeDe. "But he doesn't look like that anymore."

"What do you mean?" asked Aldo.

"He grew a moustache."

"Oh," said Aldo.

"Yes," said DeDe. "After he and my mother decided to get a divorce and my father moved away from here, he started growing a moustache. Ever since I was a baby everyone said that I looked exactly like my father. But after he grew his moustache, he looked different."

Aldo thought for a minute. "Is that why you wear your moustache?" asked Aldo, thinking aloud.

"Yes," said DeDe softly. "If I didn't wear the moustache, I wouldn't look like my father anymore."

"What does your mother say?" Aldo asked. He was confused about the connection between the divorce and the moustache. He couldn't imagine his sister Elaine, who also resembled her father, ever wearing a false moustache if Mr. Sossi decided to grow a real one.

"My mother hates it when I wear the moustache," said DeDe. "But she had a conference with Mrs. Moss and the school psychologist, and they told her to ignore it and I would stop. So now my mother pretends that I'm not wearing it anymore. But the more she pretends, the more I'm going to wear it."

"Well, what does your father say?" asked Aldo.

"He thinks it's a big joke. He even sent me a new one in the mail this week when he wrote to say he wouldn't be seeing me again this weekend. But I'm not going to wear it.

121

I'll just wear my old one." As she spoke, DeDe reached into the pocket of her jeans and put on her moustache, which she hadn't worn all day.

Then she reached for a tissue to blow her nose. Aldo thought she was going to start to cry.

"I think you're silly," said Aldo. "If your father gets bald, like my father, will you shave your head so you can still look like him?"

"Yes," said DeDe.

"No, you wouldn't," said Aldo. "And if you did you would be nuts. Suppose he gains a hundred pounds and gets very fat. Would you have to gain a hundred pounds too? It's impossible for two people to look the same unless they're identical twins."

"I've just got to look like him," said DeDe, choking back a sob.

"He's still your father even if you don't look like him. You don't look like your mother, but she's still your mother," said Aldo.

"I know," said DeDe, "but she still lives here with me."

"Well, your father will always be your father no matter where he lives."

DeDe blew her nose again, and the moustache came off into the tissue.

"You sure would look funny bald," said Aldo.

"Not so funny as you looked when you saw that you had spilled the spaghetti," said DeDe.

"I felt really awful when it happened," admitted Aldo.

"You're a messy person, aren't you?" teased DeDe. "The very first day I met you, you spilled the applesauce at school."

"It was your fault," said Aldo. "You knocked it out of my hand." But he didn't speak with anger. He was having a good time talking with DeDe. He finally knew her secret, and, even more important, he knew for sure now that they were going to be friends.

"I should bring Cookie to school," said

DeDe, laughing. "She could get a job in the lunchroom, cleaning up spilled food."

"That's right. Like raw eggs," said Aldo.

Aldo and DeDe laughed together.

"One morning I made myself a health shake in the blender for my breakfast. I forgot to put the cover on before I pushed the button. There was milk and honey and egg on the wall and on the ceiling and all over my sister Elaine," Aldo recalled. "Cookie couldn't have licked that up."

"Do you really think my father will still love me, even if I don't look like him anymore?" asked DeDe abruptly.

"Sure," said Aldo. "I like you and you don't look like me."

"Who'd want to look like you?" said DeDe, grinning.

"Don't insult me," said Aldo, grinning back at her. "Or else the next time I bring applesauce to school, I'll spill it all over you."

"You wouldn't dare," said DeDe, laughing.

"Yes, I would," insisted Aldo. "They don't call me Applesauce for nothing."

The rest of the afternoon passed too quickly. DeDe showed him pictures that her father had taken at the bird sanctuary. It was nearby, and DeDe promised to show him where they had seen the nest of goose eggs last spring. Aldo hadn't known that Canada geese came to live in New Jersey every spring, and he was eager to see them. Woodside was certainly an interesting place, and there were a lot of things he could do with DeDe now that the afternoons were getting longer and warmer.

When he put his jacket on before he went home, he again felt the moustache in his pocket. Aldo pulled it out and said, "I wasn't trying to tease you last week. Do you want this?"

DeDe colored. "No," she said. Then she put her hand in her own pocket and pulled out the moustache that she had been wearing earlier. "I don't even think I need this one, anymore." She held it out to Aldo. "Here. You can have it."

For a second, Aldo looked at the moustache in DeDe's hand.

"Really?" he asked.

"Listen, Applesauce, I wouldn't say it if I didn't mean it," said DeDe.

Aldo grabbed the moustache out of DeDe's hand and stuffed it into his pocket with his own. He didn't need it, but neither did DeDe, and he thought he should take it before she changed her mind.

"You know what?" said DeDe.

"What?" asked Aldo.

DeDe giggled. "My father *is* starting to get bald!"

A cold March wind was blowing when Aldo went outside and started walking home. But even though the temperature had dropped many degrees since the morning, Aldo was feeling very warm and good inside.

His fingers in his pocket played with the two moustaches. They were the best proof of all that DeDe was his special friend. He was glad his family had moved to Woodside. When the ground got warmer, Aldo was going to help his father plant a vegetable garden. He knew that gardening would be interesting, and maybe DeDe would like to help them too. It would be fun.

As he walked the last block toward his house, Aldo passed a boy on the street.

"Hi, Applesauce!" the boy called.

Instead of cringing or ignoring him, Aldo turned to look at the boy. He grinned. It was Michael Frank.

"Hi, Frankfurter!" he responded.

Vegetarians might not eat frankfurters, thought Aldo, but he could certainly say the word.

"See you at school on Monday, Applesauce," said Michael.

"OK, Frankfurter," said Aldo.

And he walked on home to Hillside La.

Born in New York City, Johanna Hurwitz received a B.A. at Queens College and an M.S. in Library Science from Columbia University. Formerly a children's librarian with the New York Public Library, Mrs. Hurwitz has worked in a variety of library positions in New York and Long Island. She lives in Great Neck, New York, with her husband, two children, and a cat.

Although Mrs. Hurwitz's books for boys and girls are fictitious, she admits to having put at least one cake failure out in her backyard for the birds and squirrels to eat. They loved it.

John Wallner was born in St. Louis, Missouri, where he earned a B.F.A. in painting and graphics from Washington University. He also has an M.F.A. in graphics and art history from Pratt Institute in Brooklyn, New York. In addition to illustrating many award-winning children's books, Mr. Wallner has lectured and taught. His honors include exhibition in shows at the Corcoran School of Art in Washington, D.C., and the Society of Illustrators. In 1977, he received the Friends of American Writers Award for Best Juvenile Illustrator.

Mr. Wallner and his wife live in Ossining, New York.